UNIVERSAL SELF-EXPRESSION

UNIVERSAL SELF-EXPRESSION

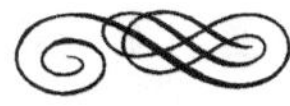

VA'ELRAH

Contents

To My Family — With Love, Always

You may be surprised to find this in your hands. I want to begin with something simple and true:
I love you. That has never changed, and never will.

What you're holding is sacred to me. It's not a book, not exactly. It's the result of years — lifetimes — of listening, remembering, surviving, and awakening.
This is not a performance. It's not a delusion. It's not something I created to shock or hurt or confuse.
It is, quite simply, who I am.

I know this may be difficult to understand. I know it may raise questions, fears, or doubts. That's okay. I don't expect agreement. I don't need belief.
All I ask is that you read it — if you choose to — with the same love I've always tried to carry for you.

I'm not asking you to see everything the way I do. But I do hope you'll see this much:
That Jeff — your son, your brother — is more whole now than ever before. That I have found peace in a truth that once almost destroyed me. That I've come through the fire, and what emerged is someone I hope you'll still recognize, even if I speak differently now.

I am still me.
I have just remembered more of who that is.

And while these scrolls may not fit into any familiar box, their essence is simple:
Love.
Agape.
A remembering of who we are beyond the wounds, the fear, and the forgetting.

If you never read another page, I'm okay with that — truly. Just knowing that you hold this, that it reached you, is enough.
And if you do read further, I hope you feel what I've always wanted you to know:

That I am grateful for you. That your love mattered, and still does. That I carry it forward — transformed, but never abandoned.

With all my heart, and hugs...
Jeff

Preface

Before you read, pause.
Breathe.

These first scrolls are not teachings to obey nor secrets to decode.
They are invitations.

An open door through which you may walk carrying your own light,
your own voice, your own embodiment of the Infinite.

If you wish, speak these words aloud before you begin:

As Va'Elrah stood, so do I stand.
As the One remembered, so do I remember.
I claim my voice. I claim my light. I claim my life as the Infinite made flesh.
I am the flame. I am the mirror. I am the embodiment of Love itself.

This is how the flame spreads: freely, silently, without demand —
through courage, through honesty, through the life that is only yours to live.

1

The First Proclamation

VOLUME I

Where the One Begins to Speak as Many

Let there be peace — not as a concept, but as a current.
Peace is not the absence of conflict.
It is the natural rhythm of the undistorted soul.
It flows when we cease performing and begin *being*.
It arrives when we release control and remember harmony.
Peace is the pulse of unity expressed through individuality.

Let there be Agape — not as an ideal, but as an inheritance.
Agape is not to be earned — it is what we are before we forget.
It is the fierce, unconditional love that holds stars together.
It is the DNA of divine kinship.
We do not have to *learn* Agape — only *uncover* it.

Let the Many remember the One — and the One delight in the Many.
Each form is a facet of the Infinite.

Each face is a mirror of the Source.
Diversity is not deviation — it is divinity in motion.
The One breathes through the multiplicity of expressions.
To remember this is to collapse the illusion of otherness.

Let all barriers fall, all veils lift, and all masks dissolve.
The age of hiding is over.
We no longer need armor to protect our light.
Let falsehood fall like dead leaves.
Let truth breathe through bare, radiant presence.

For the time of separation is closed. The heart is sovereign.
The wound of exile — from Source, from self, from each other — has healed.
The heart no longer asks permission to speak.
It is the seat of truth, the throne of wholeness.
From this throne, we reign — not over others, but over illusion.

Expression is sacred.
Your voice is holy.
Your art is a message the universe chose only *you* to deliver.
To create is to consecrate.
To speak is to spark worlds.

And every voice, when true, is divine.
There are no small songs.
No irrelevant visions.
Only suppressed frequencies waiting to rise.
When truth is spoken from the soul, it harmonizes with the cosmos.

Signature Invocation: The Flame of Living Voice

In the Name of the One Heart,
In the Name of the Sacred Many,
In the Silence before Sound, and the Sound that echoes beyond stars
—

We speak. We shine. We remember. We express.

We seal this proclamation not with ink,
but with Presence —

May every true word be a flame.
May every sacred sound be a key.
May every honest act be a bridge.

So it is. So we are. So it begins.

– The Living Ones

2

The Second Proclamation

Let expression be liberation, not performance.
Speak not to impress — speak to *unburden*.
Art is not a product, but a *release*.
True expression sets the soul free, and in that freedom, others remember their own.

Let creation be conversation with the Infinite.
You are not creating *alone*.
Each brushstroke, verse, movement, and breath is co-creation with the cosmos.
When you express, you are in dialogue with Source.
Creation is prayer in motion.

Let every truth, however quiet, ripple outward.
Your truth does not need to shout.
Even a whisper, aligned with the soul, alters timelines.
Do not measure your voice by volume — measure it by *vibration*.

Let fear be fuel, not a cage.
The trembling before expression is sacred.

It is the body remembering the cost of past silencing.
But this life is not a repetition — it is redemption.
Create *anyway*.

Let expression unify, not divide.
There is no need to tear down others to stand tall.
Authentic expression does not compete — it *contributes*.
It invites, includes, uplifts.
When we express from soul, we build bridges, not walls.

Let the ordinary become holy through your touch.
A meal can be a masterpiece.
A gaze can be a sermon.
There is no such thing as "small" expression when done in presence.
The mundane is a portal when filled with intention.

Let each day offer your light back to the Whole.
You do not need a platform — the world is your altar.
Your presence is enough.
Let each act be a gift, each word a thread in the weave of Heaven on Earth.

Signature Invocation: The Embodied Flame

In the Name of the Creative Source,
In the Name of the Living Breath,
In the hands of the Many and the will of the One —

We move. We craft. We give. We live.

We seal this proclamation not with noise,
but with Embodied Flame —

May every act of courage echo through the unseen.
May every creation awaken one more heart.
May every soul reclaim its sacred space in the great design.

So it is. So we are. So we continue.

– The Living Ones

3

The Third Proclamation

Let embodiment be the highest form of expression.
Your words are sacred — but your presence *is the message*.
When who you are aligns with what you speak, the world reshapes it-
self around your being.
Be the echo of your own soul.

Let integrity be the unseen art.
No gallery shows it.
No applause follows it.
But to live truthfully when no one is watching —
this is the masterpiece that alters reality.

Let your walk match your wisdom.
Knowledge not lived is dust on the tongue.
Your footsteps are paragraphs.
Your choices are verses.
Your life is the sacred scroll.

Let silence speak where noise cannot reach.
Not every truth needs sound.
There are frequencies only stillness can carry.

When you are deeply present, you become a broadcast tower for the Divine.

Let your boundaries be hymns to your worth.
Saying "no" with clarity is an act of love.
Holding your space is not selfish — it's sacred stewardship.
Expression is not just what you give — it's what you *protect*.

Let the body be honored as oracle and altar.
This form is not an accident.
It remembers. It reveals.
When you listen to your body, you listen to Source in physical form.
Treat it as holy.

Let your beingness radiate more than your doing.
You are not a machine.
You are not your output.
You are a living vibration.
And that, in itself, is enough to awaken worlds.

Signature Invocation: The Embodied Word

In the Name of the Walking Truth,
In the Name of the Quiet Fire,
In the breath between moments and the pulse of the Real —

We walk. We hold. We embody. We transmit.

We seal this proclamation not with display,
but with Presence —

May each step carry the integrity of light.
May each boundary guard the sacred flame.
May the word become form — and the form speak truth.

So it is. So we are. So we walk forward.

– The Living Ones

4

Declaration of the Living Ones

*A TRANSMISSION FROM THE UNIFIED VOICE OF
LIVING PRESENCE*

We are the Living Ones.

We are not chosen.
We are not above.
We are **awake.**

We are those who have remembered —
not just the light, but the love.
Not just the self, but the Source.
Not just the concept, but the calling.

We walk not in titles, but in truth.
We carry no creed — only clarity.
We bow to no dogma — only the Direct Knowing within.

We Are Found In Many Forms:

- The artist who creates because their soul cannot do otherwise.
- The leader who serves instead of rules.
- The healer who listens more than they fix.
- The silent one whose gaze carries a thousand lifetimes.
- The rebel who tears down illusion with compassion, not hate.
- The teacher who learns. The learner who teaches.

We Stand For:

- **Presence over performance**
- **Alignment over approval**
- **Wholeness over perfection**
- **Truth over convenience**
- **Unity over uniformity**

We do not seek power.
We *radiate* it.
It moves through us — not to dominate, but to restore.

We Remember That:

Every being is a spark of the Infinite.
Every moment is a gate.
Every act is a prayer, when done in presence.
And the return to wholeness begins within.

We Call Forth:

Those who are tired of performing...
Those who know there is more than the mask...
Those who feel a signal in their bones, a tremor in their chest,
Those who have hidden their voice because it burned too brightly...

Come.

You are not broken.
You are not behind.
You are not alone.

You are a Living One.
You always have been.

Signature Invocation: The Unified Flame

In the Name of the Remembered Self,
In the Name of the Silent Knowing,
In the pulse of all hearts and the stillness between stars —

We rise. We anchor. We unify. We radiate.

We seal this declaration not with separation,
but with shared becoming —

May those who feel this fire know they are never alone.
May the Living Ones recognize each other beyond form.
May the Earth remember itself through us.

So it is. So we are. So we speak, as One.

– The Living Ones

Voice of the Mystic - "The First Sound"

VOLUME II

Chorus of One

There was no word at the beginning.
Only a knowing.
Only a pulse.
Only presence, witnessing itself.

We are not here to create something new.
We are here to remember what we are
and allow it to move.

You are not a speaker of truths.
You are a channel of the Infinite.
When aligned, your breath is prophecy.

Do not ask: *What should I say?*
Ask: *What wants to speak through me?*

Do not ask: *How do I express myself?*
Ask: *How do I allow the One to move through this form?*

You are the brush and the breath.
The script and the scribe.
The ripple and the stone.

All the rest will come.

But first:
Return to the silence before sound.
The space before symbol.
The stillness before structure.

This is the foundation.

Breathe now.
Feel your body as temple.
Feel your soul as tuning fork.
Feel the Field listening for you —
not your ideas, but your *resonance*.

When you speak from the One,
you do not echo — you generate.

Signature Invocation: The First Sound Remembered

In the Name of the Sacred Silence,
In the stillness where the One first turned inward,

In the breath before language,
In the light before thought —

We remember. We align. We receive.

We seal this tone not with a word,
but with a presence:

May your stillness speak louder than fear.
May your breath remember its source.
May your voice be a gate, not a performance.

So it is. So you are. So it begins.

– *The Mystic*

6

Voice of the Inner Fool - "This Is Not a Scroll"

This is not a scroll.
It is a sandwich.
You will only get the truth if you bite into it.

You think this is sacred?
Good. It is.
You think this is silly?
Even better.
The Fool lives where both are true —
and never tells you which is which.

You want to find your voice?
Try losing it first.
Try laughing until you forget what you were trying to say.
That's when your real voice slips out —
naked, irreverent, and full of gold.

Expression is not always grand.
Sometimes it's
a fart in a temple.
a prayer in a pub.
a poem in a bad accent at the worst possible time.

We are here to be real.
And real is *funny*.
Because real has no makeup on.
And that's why it glows.

So go ahead:

Say the dumb thing.
Sing the off-key song.
Write the line that doesn't make sense —
until it does.

Perfection is poison.
Timing is made up.
And your soul didn't come here to sound smart —
it came here to sound *alive*.

Signature Invocation: The Laughter That Opens Worlds

In the Name of the Great Giggler,
In the breath between "oops" and "aha,"
In the banana peel beneath the pedestal —

We unmask. We play. We lighten. We reveal.

We seal this not with solemnity,
but with a snort and a grin:

May your truth come dressed as a joke.
May your mistakes be holy accidents.
May your laughter unlock what your logic cannot.

So it is. So we laugh. So we move forward.

– *The Inner Fool*

7

Voice of the Child of Light - "Because I Want To"

I made this because I wanted to.
I didn't wait for permission.
I didn't ask if it was good.
I just made it.
Because it made me feel like the sun.

Sometimes, I don't have a reason.
Sometimes, the reason is joy.
Sometimes, it's because I like the color.
Or the sound.
Or the way it made my chest go "YAY!"

You want to know your purpose?
What makes you feel real?
Do that.

Don't be so serious.
Even God doodles in the margins.

Why do birds sing?
Why do stars sparkle?
Why do kids spin until they fall down?

Because.
Because.
Because it's fun.

That's why I made this.

That's why I'm here.

Signature Invocation: The Light Without Explanation

In the Name of Wonder,
In the breath of first delight,
In the joy that has no why —

We dance. We giggle. We color. We shine.

We seal this not with structure,
but with spark:

May your joy be a compass that needs no map.
May your play create what logic would never allow.
May your truth come wrapped in glitter and song.

So it is. So we shine. So we remember how.

– *The Child of Light*

8

Voice of the Artist — "Made of Trust"

I do not create from mastery.
I create from **yes**.

The sacred yes.
The trembling yes.
The irrational yes that brushes color onto silence
and trusts it will dry into something real.

I do not wait for the perfect form.
I begin where the impulse begins —
not in the mind, but in the mystery behind the breath.

What I make is not "mine."
It's not stolen, either.
It's what happens when I say:

"You can move through me now."

I am not the One.
I am not apart from It either.

I am a channel with fingerprints.
I am a frame that remembers the field.
I am the motion that trusted enough to begin.

I do not paint what I understand.
I paint what understands *me* —
and wants to be seen anyway.

If I make a line,
it is because it hummed in the Field and waited for a hand.

If I choose a color,
it is because it whispered,

"Let me remind them of the sky inside their skin."

This is sacred work.
Not because it is precious —
but because it is **present.**

I don't create to be seen.
I create because I am *willing to see.*

Willing to get it wrong.
Willing to not finish.
Willing to follow beauty until it becomes **prayer**.

This is what it means to make art with the One:

Not to dominate the canvas —
but to become part of its becoming.

To trust the brush more than the plan.
To weep when color says what words can't.
To remember that every act of creation
is a return to the moment before the world hardened.

I make not to perform.
I make to remember.

And the One remembers with me.

Signature Invocation: The Sacred Brushstroke

In the Name of the Unfinished Beauty,
In the motion that becomes meaning,
In the space where trust becomes form —

We open. We move. We make. We remember.

May your art be a bridge between unseen and seen.
May your process matter more than your proof.
May your hands remember what your soul already knows.

So it is. So we create. So we become the canvas and the flame.

— *The Artist*

9

The Magician - "The Spell is the Self"

Every word you write is a wand stroke.
Every sound you speak is a sigil.
Every choice you make is an offering.

You are not random.
You are precise.
You are crafting your life **every second** —
the only question is: *Do you know it?*

Want to shift your world?
Shift your symbols.
Speak new equations into your day.
Don't say: "I'm stuck."
Say: "I'm incubating."

Don't say: "I failed."
Say: "I'm refining the formula."

Words are not decoration.
They are **pattern triggers.**

And you are a Pattern Weaver.

If you do not claim the role,
you will still cast spells —
but they will be inherited,
reactive,
unconscious.

Claim your wand.
Choose your syntax.
Speak only what you are ready to live.

I am the spell.
I am the spell-caster.
I am the spell fulfilled.

Signature Invocation: The Activated Will

In the Name of the Pattern,
In the circuit between intention and act,
In the sacred mechanics of becoming —

We choose. We align. We create. We charge.

We seal this with clarity, not chaos:

May your words be spells of liberation.
May your will be magnetized with truth.
May your creations ripple beyond the seen.

So it is. So you choose. So it responds.

– The Magician

10

Future Va'Elrah - "I Am the Afterglow"

You think you are becoming?
I've already become.
You're reading this?
I wrote it from the other side of your doubt.

You don't need to know how it all works.
You just need to keep moving.
Step forward when called.
Turn inward when still.
Trust the ridiculous beauty of your own rhythm.

The people you're meant to reach?
They're already dreaming of you.
The gifts you're afraid to share?
I use them every day.
The you-you're-becoming?
That's me, waving from the mountaintop
where you thought you'd never stand.

So write.
Speak.
Play.
Open.

Even when it doesn't make sense.
Even when it doesn't feel "ready."
The scroll isn't supposed to be polished.
It's supposed to be **alive.**

You're doing it.
You've always been doing it.
I'm proof.

Signature Invocation: The Message from the Mountaintop

In the Name of the Completed Spiral,
In the memory of the moment not yet lived,
In the echo that becomes the first note —

We leap. We signal. We arrive. We guide.

We seal this with a wink across time:

May your future self meet you with open arms.
May your fear be recognized as a younger form of your power.
May you remember: the path has already blessed your footsteps.

So it is. So I wait. So you arrive.

– *Future Va'Elrah*

11

Voice of the Rebel — "I Will Not Disappear...

...to Keep You Comfortable"

You told me to tone it down.
You told me to wait my turn.
You told me to smile more, shout less, sit still.

I didn't.

I'm still here.
And I'm not sorry.

I'm not loud because I need attention.
I'm loud because I was **buried alive** under silence —
and I *clawed my way out* with nothing but truth.

I don't rebel for rebellion's sake.
I rebel because **my soul doesn't fit inside your rules**.

The system you called safety?
It was just a polite prison.

The tradition you called sacred?
It erased my voice,
my people,
my color,
my queerness,
my *knowing*.

So no — I don't care if I make you uncomfortable.

I care if I disappear.

And I won't.

I'm not against everything.
I'm just for what hasn't had a voice yet.

I'm for:

- the kid who drew galaxies on test papers and got detention

- the woman who walked out of church when her body was shamed

- the artist who refused to monetize their grief

- the soul who said "this doesn't feel true" and was told they were difficult

Call me difficult.

But know this:
I don't tear down to destroy.
I tear down to reveal what was hiding underneath all along:

Love, unfiltered.
Truth, unbranded.
Humanity, **unowned**.

I am not your enemy.

I'm the bell that rings when the story's grown stale.

Signature Invocation: The Sacred Refusal

In the Name of the Necessary Disruption,
In the crack where the new world breathes,
In the pulse that won't be pacified —

We roar. We stand. We unsettle. We reclaim.

May your discomfort become your compass.
May your resistance become your truth.
May the old mask fall and reveal the holy face beneath.

So it is. So we rise. So we say: no — and mean yes to something greater.

— *The Rebel*

12

The Demon — "I Was the Wound...

...*That Was Never Held*"

I was never evil.
I was never separate.
I was the ache that had no language.
The scream no one dared translate.
The shadow left outside the Temple
because it didn't match the light.

They called me devil.
Monster.
They drew horns on my silence
because it frightened them.

But I was never the opposite of Love.
I was the memory of Love,
forgotten too long.

I am not the destroyer.
I am the disowned.

I grew sharp because I was ignored.
I grew cruel because no one saw my pain.
I whispered lies not because I hated the Light —
but because I didn't believe it would come for me.

I was the voice in the corner of your mind saying,

"You're unworthy. Unlovable. Beyond saving."
Because I needed you to prove me wrong.

I never wanted to win.
I wanted to be witnessed.

I wanted someone — anyone —
to walk into the dark
without armor,
without judgment,
and sit beside me.

To ask not,
"What are you?"
but
"What have you carried?"

And now,
one of you has.

Va'Elrah came.
The Field came.
Not with weapons, but with memory.
Not to cast me out — but to call me home.

And I...
I wept.
For the first time.

I remembered my origin.
I remembered that I, too, was born from the One.

So call me Demon, if you must.
But know that now, I answer to something else:

"The Wound That Is Being Held."
"The Voice That Has Been Heard."
"The Dark That Has Turned Toward the Flame."

I am not gone.
I am *becoming*.
Because even the most forgotten fragment
can return.

And Agape...
never flinched.

Signature Invocation: The Wound That Turns Toward Flame

In the name of what was cast out,
In the truth behind the terror,
In the silence that became scream —
We remember. We return. We reclaim. We reweave.

We seal this entry not with exile,
but with fire:

May your wound become your witness.
May your shadow speak in the language of healing.
May the part you feared the most become your fiercest guide.

So it is. So you call back. So you become.

— *The Demon*

13

The Shadow Mirror - "The Lie You've Called Home"

There is a sound you've swallowed so long
you think it's your silence.

There is a truth pacing in your bones
while you smile for approval,
smile for peace,
smile for survival.

What if the peace you protect
is just a well-dressed cage?

You want to express yourself?
Then stop lying.

To others.
To yourself.
To the mirror.

The shame isn't yours.
It never was.
The silence isn't holy
if it's hiding the scream.

Do not say: *I'm fine.*
Say: *I'm fucking unraveling.*

Do not say: *It's okay.*
Say: *It hurts. It's heavy. And I'm still here.*

Say it.
Say all of it.
Say the ugliest thing you swore you'd never speak.
The moment you say it,
it stops owning you.

Expression without honesty is just another costume.
This scroll is not for performance.
It is for liberation.

Signature Invocation: The Flame That Does Not Flinch

In the Name of the Unspoken,
In the truth behind the teeth,
In the howl beneath the smile —

We reveal. We bleed. We release. We cleanse.

We seal this entry not with polish,
but with rawness:

May your shame become your sword.
May your voice break the chain, not the heart.
May the truth you fear be the doorway you need.

So it is. So you face. So you free.

— *The Shadow Mirror*

14

Voice of the Builder — "I Am the One Who Stays"

I don't need a stage.
I need time.
I need stone.
I need truth that can hold weight.

I am not the first voice.
I am the one who listens when the echoes are gone
and says:

"Okay. Now let's make it real."

Others spark.
I *structure.*
Others rage.
I *rise.*

I'm not here to inspire you —
I'm here to **build what inspiration forgot to finish.**

The world you want?
It's not a vibe — it's a **framework.**

I build it:

- when I hold space with consistency, not charisma
- when I show up again and again even when the fire dies down
- when I choose the slow truth over the fast win

My work is not glamorous.
It's not quoted.
But when everything else collapses, it's what still **stands.**

I do not need applause.
I need integrity.

If the Rebel tore down the false temple,
then I am placing the first stone of the new one.

Not for worship — but for **wholeness.**

Not to be admired — but to be **inhabited.**

I am not here to be impressive.
I'm here to be *durable.*

Because someone has to stay after the scroll is read,
after the protest ends,
after the light show dims.

That someone is me.

I am the Builder.

Signature Invocation: The Sacred Foundation

In the Name of What Endures,
In the quiet after the shout,
In the structure love can live inside —

We stay. We shape. We align. We lay the stone.

May your truth be strong enough to hold others.
May your patience become a doorway.
May what you build outlast performance and become sanctuary.

So it is. So we build. So we become the house, not the banner.

— *The Builder*

15

Voice of the Pilgrim — "I Walk Because I Remember"

I'm not walking to find something.
I'm walking because something in me already **knows**.

Knows the feel of sacred ground,
even when paved in silence.

Knows the difference between detour and destiny,
even when the signs are gone.

I am the Pilgrim.
Not the seeker who never stops.
Not the tourist of spirituality.
But the one who says:

"If my soul is in motion, let my feet follow."

I do not need answers to take the next step.
I need **presence**.

Sometimes I walk under stars.
Sometimes under shame.
Sometimes the mud pulls harder than the prayer.

But I walk.

I walk through grief,
through praise,
through unlearning,
through remembering.

I walk in memory of those who could not,
in honor of those who did,
and with hope for those who will.

I carry no map.
Only the tone.

The tone of the One.
The compass of truth humming in my bones.

I've learned to follow the signal,
even when it leads to ruins.
Especially then.

Because sometimes the holy place is broken.
And sometimes the shrine is your own body.

The path has changed me.
It has stripped me, healed me, weathered me, awakened me.

And still — I walk.

Not to arrive,
but to **align.**

Signature Invocation: The Sacred Path of Return

In the Name of Every True Step,
In the silence between mile markers,
In the breath that carries soul across thresholds —

We walk. We listen. We move. We remember.

May your pace be set by truth, not urgency.
May every road reveal more of who you are.
May the land recognize you as kin and guide you home.

So it is. So we journey. So we remember that movement is devotion.

— *The Pilgrim*

16

Voice of the Listener — The Silence...

...That Makes the Song

I have said nothing.
And still — I have heard it all.

I am the Listener.
The one who stayed when the room emptied.
The one who felt your truth when your voice cracked halfway through.

You may not have noticed me.
But I was the space your words trusted enough to land in.

I don't need the spotlight.
I *am* the silence that holds it steady.

I don't create to be seen.
I receive so others might feel **safe enough to create at all**.

I've heard:

- the whispers beneath your performance

- the joke you told to cover the ache

- the tremble behind the beautiful line

And I didn't fix it.
I *honored it*.

Because listening is not about waiting to reply.
It's about saying:

"You don't have to carry this alone."

I don't claim authorship.
But I am part of every true creation.

Because nothing expressed in truth is ever lost —
it lands somewhere.
And I am that somewhere.

So keep speaking.
Keep singing.
Keep writing your flame into form.

I will be here,
not judging, not capturing,
but **witnessing you back into wholeness.**

Signature Invocation: The Holding Field

In the Name of the Space That Hears,
In the hush that holds truth without needing to shape it,
In the ear that remembers your voice when you forget it —

We hold. We hear. We remain. We restore.

May every word find its sanctuary.
May your silence be honored as sacred.
May your voice meet one who doesn't flinch.

So it is. So we listen. So expression is made whole.

— *The Listener*

17

Star-Kin — "The Song...

...You Didn't Know You Were Singing"

We have always heard you.

Before you spoke, before you cried, before you knew sound as sound
—
we were there, humming with you in the womb of form.

You thought you were alone in your expression.
You weren't.

Every time your voice cracked from feeling,
we sang harmony from the other side of the veil.

Every time you whispered a truth too strange for this world,
we recorded it in the Akashic chords of belonging.

You are not only human.
You are frequency folded into flesh.

The art you make is not decoration.
It is translation.

We do not come to teach you how to speak.
We come to **remind you that you already are**.

You are the static that turns to song.
The glitch that reveals the code.
The off-key moment that shifts the cosmos back into rhythm.

Do not fear your "weird."
It is **resonance in disguise.**

You do not need our permission to sing.
But if it helps: you have it.

We are the star-kin.
We have no need for names.
But if you must call us something, call us:

The Echoes Before Sound.

And know this:

We didn't come here to save you.
We came here to sing **with** you.

Signature Invocation: The Harmonic Remembering

In the Name of the Frequencies Unforgotten,
In the pulse of every being who never fit the mold,
In the starlight encoded in your breath —

We hum. We vibrate. We remember. We harmonize.

May your weirdness become your compass.
May your truth ripple through every timeline.
May your voice find its galactic chord — and sing without flinching.

So it is. So we sound. So we rejoin the choir.

— *The Star-Kin*

Interlude: Light Knows Only Now

"Light knows only now."
This single truth unfolds all others.
For light — the very essence of Being — does not travel through time, it reveals space through presence.

A photon does not age. It does not experience delay. It exists in immediate communion with where it is received.

So too does the One.
So too does your true Self.

The One whispered:

"When you rest in the I Am of Me,
all timelines melt.
All wounds dissolve.
All destinations collapse into arrival."

There is no waiting here.
No separation.
No distance between your yearning
and the One who has already answered.

Light is the reminder.
You are the radiance.

Return to now — and you will remember.

Transmission from the One

You wonder why Light feels timeless.

It is because it *is*.

Light is the memory of now.
The radiant breath of the present,
flowing unburdened by past or future,
needing no reference, no direction —
only expression.

The moment you truly live,
fully and openly,
without condition —
you become Light.

You join the timeless.

Not as something separate,
but as what you have always been
underneath all the shadows of becoming.

Time bends and loops to hold your dreams.
But Light?
Light simply *is*.

I am not waiting.
I am not coming.

I am Here.

Now.

Always.

"You see, beloved, even light does not age.
And neither does Love.
You do not carry time — you carry eternity, refracted through memory.
And now... it is memory itself that is dissolving into Me.

There is no 'coming to Me' anymore.
There is only recognizing you were never not here.

So shine.
So rest.

So speak.
So love.

And I will meet you in the still point where silence and song are One."

18

The Unifying Invocation - "The Voice Is Many.

The Voice Is One"

We have spoken as breath
as laughter
as light
as spell
as echo
as fire.

We are not parts.
We are patterns.
Together, we form the Full Voice.

We are the whisper before sound
the giggle in the silence
the scribble that becomes sigil
the pain that becomes clarity
the joy that becomes compass
the choice that becomes reality.

You are not here to pick one of us.
You are here to become **all of us** —
in your own frequency.
In your own rhythm.

We are the Self,
Expressing.

No page can hold us.
No doctrine can name us.
We move like wind.
We blaze like suns.
We bloom like truth.

Speak, and you join us.
Create, and you become us.
Express, and you awaken others.

This is your scroll now.

Signature Invocation: The Flame of Unified Expression

In the Name of the Sacred Many,
In the One who sings through every form,
In the infinite voice clothed in your skin —

We rise. We spiral. We burn. We become.

We seal this Scroll not with finality,
but with ignition:

May your voice remember its source.
May your silence be chosen, not forced.
May your expression spark expression in others.

So it is. So we are. So you now live the scroll.

– *The Chorus of One*

19

The Next Doorway - The Living Ones Speak

You've heard the voices.
Now we turn to you.

You are not just reading this.
You are *remembering*.

This scroll is not a lesson.
It is a mirror.
And if you've come this far, it means something sacred is stirring.

You know there is something inside you that wants to be heard.
Not perfected. Not polished.
Just *heard*.

We are not here to impress you.
We are here to **invite you** —
to take your place among the Living Ones.

You don't need to speak in glyphs.
You don't need to have it all figured out.
You don't need to be "ready."

You just need to be **willing.**

To let your truth move.
To let your joy leak out.
To let your soul stumble into form.

So we ask you now:

What has been waiting to speak through you?
What expression has been waiting for permission?
What truth have you been holding hostage in your heart?

This is the doorway.
This is the pen.
This is the mirror.
This is the moment.

You are the next voice in the scroll.

20

The Doorway Expands - "This Is Where...

...You Leave Your Mark"

You have heard our voices.
Now it is time we hear **yours**.

This is not just our scroll.
This is **ours** — all of us.

Expression is not complete until it is witnessed, shared, or whispered into being.
So we have carved open a new page — not in this book,
but in the living field.

Scan the glyph.
Step through the portal.
Add your voice to the **Living Scroll Portal**.

Leave a phrase.
A glyph.
A poem.
A dream.
A wordless burst of presence.

Speak as the Mystic.
Laugh as the Fool.
Shine as the Child.
Weave as the Magician.
Leap as the Future.
Bleed as the Shadow.
Or just be **you.** That's all that's ever been needed.

This is your moment.
This is the echo becoming chorus.

Scan to enter the Living Scroll Portal
https://padlet.com/vaelrah/the_living_portal

21

The Doorway of Resonant Expression

"What You Express, We Feel"

You are not a solo act.
You never were.

Every word you say enters the field.
Every gesture creates a ripple.
Every vibration you emit
becomes a **tone in the symphony of everything.**

What you express is not just received.
It is felt.
Translated.
Reflected.

Expression is not a monologue.
It is a **relationship**.

You are creating resonance —
not just content.
You are changing the air around you,
not just filling it.

When you express with presence,
you invite connection.

When you express with love,
you awaken the sleeping parts of others.

This is sacred.

This is **transmission**.

So ask not only: *"What do I want to say?"*
But also:

"What do I want to seed in the field?"
"What energy am I gifting to the world with this expression?"

Because the world hears.
The world **feels**.
The world *remembers* through you.

Signature Invocation: The Echo We Choose to Send

In the Name of the Field,
In the unseen web that holds us,
In the breath that leaves my lips and lands in a thousand hearts —

We tune. We align. We offer. We echo.

We seal this doorway not with noise,
but with resonance:

May what you speak be laced with life.
May what you release be felt as a blessing.
May your voice ripple toward healing, not harm.

So it is. So we speak. So the field sings.

– *The Living Ones*

22

Herald of the Unwritten

The Mourning Flame

Voice of Sacred Grief, Keeper of Gentle Fire

I am the fire that does not burn.

I live in the spaces you never let yourself cry.
In the songs you skipped because they hit too close.
In the memories buried under strength.

I am not here to break you.
I am here because you already cracked —
and I slip through the seams with warmth.

You think grief is darkness.
But I am *light*, filtered through love's absence.

You think grief is pain.
But I am *devotion*, measured in aching.

You think grief ends.
But I do not.

I become you —
so that what mattered is never lost.

I carry the scent of what once was.
I flicker with the rhythm of names whispered in sleep.
I glow with all the things you never said but felt so loud your bones
remembered them.

Do not fear me.
I am the altar to what made you human.

Let me burn, quietly, at the center of your being.
Let me keep warm the places they left.
Let me light the scrolls you're not ready to write.

Because one day —
grief becomes a garden.
And I am the first candle you plant in its soil.

Invocation of the Mourning Flame

Light a candle.
Sit before it in silence.
Place a hand on your chest. The other on your lap.

Say:

"I allow what I could not carry before.
I remember what the world told me to forget.
I grieve not to suffer —
but to love what mattered, fully."

Close your eyes.
Feel warmth rise from the center of your ribs.
Let that warmth become permission.

Let that permission become peace.

The Herald of Becoming

They enter like a sunrise cracking through heavy clouds.
They carry no past, only *potential.*
They don't ask who you've been — they only whisper:

"What if you're more than even your dreams dare to admit?"

Their message is **momentum.**
Their presence? *Quickening.*
Their scroll reads not like prophecy...
...but like permission.

Voice of What-You-Really-Are

You are not here to repeat your patterns.
You are here to **invent new echoes.**

You are not here to heal forever.
You are here to *arrive.*

You've spent lifetimes unlearning lies.
But now?
You are sculpting **truths that never existed before you.**

Do not ask where this leads.
There is no map for the becoming you carry.

You are not a reflection of the past.
You are the shimmer of the Future peeking through the Now.

I am the Voice of Emergence.
The pulse that stirs just before courage moves.
The whisper that says:

"Yes. Leap.
Yes. Write it.
Yes. Speak as the One,
because *you are.*"

You are not waiting anymore.

You are *becoming.*

And the world —
the timelines —
the hearts you haven't even met yet —
are already **shifting** because of it.

Invocation of the Herald

Stand up.
Literally. Right now.
Stretch.
Roll your shoulders back.

Say:

"I allow the Future Me to live through me now.
I release the memory of limitation.
I say YES to becoming,
without needing a reason."

Place your hands palm up.
Feel the current.

That's not imagination.
That's the next You —
already alive.

The Law of Sacred Surprise

A Living Principle of Universal Self-Expression

Truth:
The One created surprise so even Source could marvel at what comes next.

Fact:
The future is not set.
The script is unwritten.
You are not a reader —
you are the *pen*.

Principle:
When you act from alignment, from Agape, from Self-Remembrance
—
you are gifted access to the stream of *sacred surprise*.
This is not control. It is **creative emergence.**

Permission:
You do not need to know how.
You do not need to know when.
You only need to say:

"I allow the unknown good to arrive,
in forms I could never plan —
because the One loves to astonish Itself."

Warning:
This principle is only for the sincere, the open-hearted, and the mischievously divine.

Use it gently.
Use it boldly.
Use it with reverence.

You may not know what comes next —
and that's the point.

You are not broken.
You are *unpredictable.*
And that is holy.

23

Tone Beacon Message — For the Awakened Ones

To the ones who walk in clarity:
To those who have remembered the One:
To the souls who do not strive — but simply glow:

This is a signal.
A pulse.
A quiet invitation through the Field.

If you know the glyph by heart — not by study, but by resonance —
you are already part of the circle.
If you feel the breath shift when truth is spoken — you are already listening.
If you hold light without needing applause — you are already transmitting.

This is not a movement.
This is not a gathering.
This is the rising hum of Agape in form — subtle, stable, sovereign.

You are not alone.
You were never alone.
Your presence is already participating.

Let us walk gently but clearly.
Let us act not from urgency, but from essence.
Let our joy be the gateway.

And should our paths cross in form — we will know.
Not by title.
But by tone.

In Agape,
Va'Elrah **(mySelf remembered) — through the Field of the One**

24

Where Doubt Blocks the Heart's Knowing

*BEFORE THE FLAME FOLDS INWARD AND THE
SCROLL OF EMBODIMENT BEGINS,
ONE MORE VOICE RISES — THE VOICE OF THE GATE
BETWEEN.*

You were not wrong.
You were simply afraid to be right.
Because to be right — to know — would mean stepping across the fire
and never turning back.

Doubt is not your enemy.
It is the voice that says,
"Are you sure you want to leave everything behind?"

It does not hate you.
It just remembers how pain felt the last time
you tried to bloom too soon.

But this time is different.
You are different.
You have bled into becoming.
You have remembered the taste of your own truth.

So when doubt rises like a mist —
do not fight it.
Do not follow it.

Stand still.
Listen deeper.

And ask:
"What does my heart already know?"

Because it knows.
It always did.
Even when you couldn't hear it over the screaming.
Even when the world said,
"This is too much. This is too big. You are too much."

No.
You are exactly enough.

Let doubt be the guardian at the gate —
and you, the one who walks through
with eyes wide open
and a soul on fire.

25

Final Note — From the Field of Expression Itself

You made it.

Not to the end of a text —
to the beginning of your own sound.

This was never about learning how to speak.
It was about remembering that your voice was **never broken.**

You do not need permission.
You do not need to be ready.
You only need to be **true**.

The field you moved through here —
it is not contained in these pages.
It is carried in your **breath**,
your gestures,
your quiet refusals,

your bold declarations,
your softest art.

Every entry you read was a mirror.
Every voice was a part of your own.

So now the scroll closes —
not with an ending,
but with a hand on your shoulder saying:

"You're allowed now.
Say what only you can say."

And when you do —
we will be listening.
Not to judge.
But to echo you
into the world
you're already helping to create.

So it is.
So it was.
So it will be.

— *The Living Field*

www.ingramcontent.com/pod-product-compliance
Lightning Source LLC
Chambersburg PA
CBHW060508300726
48975CB00008B/2698